The Snow of Ohreeganu

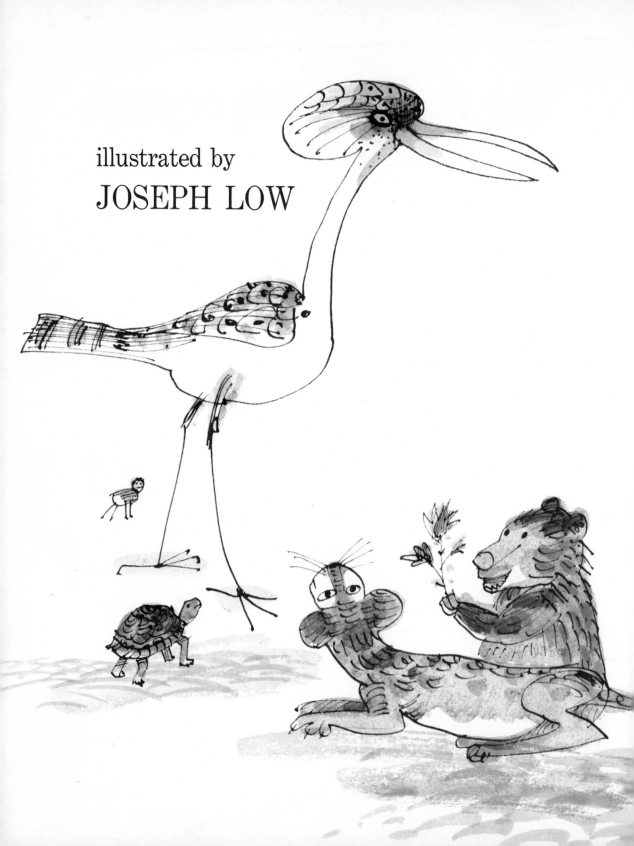

illustrated by

JOSEPH LOW

The Snow of Ohreeganu

RUSSELL E. ERICKSON

Lothrop, Lee & Shepard Co. | New York

Erickson, Russell E.
   The snow of Ohreeganu.

SUMMARY: The elephant and the mouse help
the lion keep his reckless promise to bring snow
to a nearby village.
   [1. Animals—Fiction] I. Low, Joseph, 1911-
illus. II. Title.
PZ10.3.E68Sn   [E]   73-14697
ISBN: 0-688-41539-3
ISBN: 0-688-51539-8 (lib. bdg.)

1 2 3 4 5 78 77 76 75 74

Something very unusual happened in the jungle.
No one had ever seen anything like it before and most
likely ever would again.

It happened in the village of Ohreeganu. One day a
strange bird suddenly dropped out of the sky—a large
white bird who said that he was traveling south and had
become slightly lost.

Right away the lion, being king of the jungle and leader
of the village, told the bird what to do.

"Just follow the railroad tracks outside the village. They will lead you south until you find your way again," he said happily. He loved being the center of attention.

Then the children of the village began asking the bird what it was like, where he had been and where he was going. The bird told them of many wonderful places he had seen. But what excited the children most was when he told of the Northland and its snow. They listened in amazement as he described it—how it was all fluffy and soft and so much fun to play in.

Even the grown-up animals listened attentively as he told of skis that swooshed downhill like the wind. Then he told of tobogganing, and the animals held tightly to one another as he described the thrill of skittering around icy curves. His story of a merry ride on a sled brought smiles to the faces of even the eldest animals. Then he said he must be going, and off he flew.

The children ran around the lion all shouting at once,
"We want snow! We want snow! Please bring us some
snow."

Now the lion, although he was a very good ruler and a
very kind ruler, was also a very vain ruler. Never, never
would he admit that there was anything he could not do.
So instead of saying he could not bring snow, he only said,
"I'll see, I'll see."

The next day, when he **was** asked about the snow, he said, "In a few days. In a few days."

When he said that, even the grown-ups became excited. Immediately everyone began preparing for snow. They remembered what the bird had told them. Some built sleds using slabs of wood split from logs with ironlike reeds for runners. Others made skis using only the straightest branches that were brought down by the monkeys. And a few wove mats from strong vines and shaped them into toboggans.

The lion knew then that he was in real trouble. He began staying away from the village as much as possible. He lost his appetite. He soon looked as bad as he felt. Still, he would not admit that he knew absolutely no way to bring snow to the jungle.

One hot day he took a long walk down to the river. He stopped under the bridge that the trains ran over. In the cool water a huge elephant was splashing and sloshing about, while beside him a little gray mouse was floating contentedly on his back.

When the mouse saw how sad the lion looked he came right out of the water. The elephant followed close behind.

"Hello," squeaked the mouse as he shook himself off.

The elephant tossed his trunk in a friendly wave.

"We were just passing by on our summer vacation trip," said the mouse, "and we stopped to cool off a bit before going on."

"That's nice," said the lion gloomily.

"Is something the matter?" the mouse asked. "You look sadder than my birthday cake the day my big friend here sneezed on it."

"I don't think anyone as small as you would understand a problem such as mine," said the lion. As soon as he said it he was sorry—he could see that he had hurt the mouse's feelings. The big elephant was scowling at him. "Oh, all right," said the lion, and he proceeded to tell the mouse all about the big white bird and his stories of snow and how everyone was expecting him to bring snow to the jungle.

When he finished, the mouse
was slowly shaking his
tiny head. "You certainly have a
bad snow problem," he said.

"I certainly do," said the lion, and he turned toward the
jungle.

"Wait," shouted the mouse. "If you will stay a while,
perhaps I can think of a solution to your snow problem."

The lion thought quickly. He really didn't want to stay
any longer, because he knew that if he—king of the jungle
and leader of the village—could think of no way to bring
snow, then certainly a tiny, gray puff of a mouse could not.
But still he did not want to hurt the mouse's feelings
again, so with a big sigh he went back to the river.

"Now you must be very quiet," said the mouse.

Then the lion, the mouse, and the elephant sat down on the sand and stared silently into the cool flowing water. A minute passed . . . then an hour . . . then two hours. No one made a sound as the mouse thought and thought.

Just as the sun disappeared behind the tall trees and all the jungle was in twilight, the evening train chugged slowly over the bridge.

Suddenly the mouse's whiskers began to twitch.
He jumped up. "I have just found the answer to your
snow problem!" he cried.

"Oh?" said the lion in a very doubtful tone.

"Yes, yes," squeaked the mouse. "Please go home now
and have a good night's sleep, for tomorrow there will be
snow in the jungle."

"Fine," said the lion, not believing for an instant that
this tiny gray mouse could really bring snow. He started
back to the village.

When he was gone the elephant said, "And now, my little friend, may I ask just how you think you can bring snow to the jungle?"

"Well," said the mouse, "did you see what that train was pulling as it passed over the bridge?"

The elephant scratched his head with his trunk. "Oh yes, now I remember. In fact, now that I think of it I don't believe I have ever seen so much . . . so . . . so-o-o . . ." The elephant's eyes opened wide. "Now wait a minute, you don't mean—?"

The little mouse was excitedly hopping up and down. "Oh yes, I do, oh yes, I do," he giggled. "Now pick me up, please. We have much to do tonight."

The elephant scooped the mouse up on the tip of his long trunk and set him gently on top of his head.

"Now we are going to the train yard," said the mouse. "But first we must stop at our secret diamond cave. We will need four of the biggest and finest diamonds there." As the little mouse whispered the rest of his plan into one great floppy ear, the elephant lumbered off into the darkening shadows.

Much later, when pale beams of moonlight were falling on the sleeping jungle, they arrived at the train yard. Out of a sack the mouse took four enormous diamonds. In the light of the moon they shimmered and sparkled like a million golden fireflies.

"We must put these where they will be found in the morning. They will more than pay for what we are going to need tonight," said the mouse. He then carefully hung the sack on the knob of the ticket taker's door. "Now we must go over there," he said, pointing to the railroad cars that had passed over the bridge that evening.

When they came to the cars the elephant lifted the mouse high into the air. "Hmm, I see each one is a different color," said the mouse. "Well, that will make things even better. And now, if you can remember the way, we must get to the top of that very windy mountain we came down this morning. And we must get there as quickly as possible."

The mighty elephant put his broad head against one end of the cars and began to push. He pushed harder and harder and harder, until slowly the wheels began to turn.

"Hooray!" squeaked the mouse. "Now, on to the mountain!"

As they pushed through the night the mouse, perched
high on the elephant's back, sang a little song:

> Thumpa ka-lumpa ka-rump
> My faithful friend and I
> Are climbing to the sky.
> Bumpa ka-dumpa ka-thump
> And if the wind does blow
> Tonight we'll make it snow.

Then the elephant sang a song. Then the mouse began telling funny stories. Once the elephant laughed so hard that great tears rolled down his face and he nearly stepped off the narrow winding path.

Before they knew it, they were at the very top of the mountain. The wind was blowing so fiercely that the tiny mouse could scarcely keep from being blown off the elephant's back. His whiskers and tail stood straight out.

"Can you hear me?" he shouted above the roar of the wind.

The elephant nodded.

"All right then," cried the mouse. "Open the doors! Let's make snow!"

The elephant passed his trunk slowly over the side of the first railroad car, searching for the handle. Then he saw it—the smooth metal glistened in a spot of moonlight, just beneath some fancy lettering that said:

FIRST QUALITY
❋ Extra Fine ❋ Grade A ❋
Powdered
SUGAR

The elephant slid back the heavy doors. As soon as he did, the finely powdered sugar began swirling out and, carried on the strong wind, drifted higher and higher into the night sky. Then the next car was opened, and then the next. The sky became filled with powdered sugar, and it all drifted toward the far side of the valley—to the sleeping village of Ohreeganu.

At last all of the cars were empty. The weary elephant began pushing the empty cars back to the train yard. The little mouse was so tired he fell fast asleep right in the middle of a song.

And as the mouse slept, and as the night birds sang, and as the stars twinkled, far away over Ohreeganu the powdered sugar began to fall.

The next morning the lion awakened much earlier than usual. He didn't know why at first. Then he realized it was because of all the commotion going on outside. He heard happy and excited sounds of children shouting and playing new games. Then, from the first grown-ups to arise, he heard oohs and ahs of wonderment. He rushed to his doorway to see what was happening. He blinked. He was dazzled by what he saw.

The village was breathtakingly beautiful. During
the night the powdered sugar that had fallen had
covered everything. It had changed the village into a
wonderland—a wonderland of sugar snow. Blue snow,
orange snow, green snow, and mounds and mounds
of brilliant white snow. It was the most beautiful sight
anyone had ever seen.

The new sleds and skis and toboggans were quickly
brought out. Grown-ups and little ones alike went skiing
and sliding. They rolled in the snow. They jumped in
the snow. Everyone loved it.

And enjoying the sugar snow along with everyone else
were the mouse and the elephant. The mouse would slide
down the trunk of his big friend and, giggling and
squeaking, fly off into a fluffy hill of sugar snow. Then the
elephant would blow great puffs of different colors high
into the air, and they would laugh and laugh.

The animals of the village were overjoyed, and they filled the air with songs—songs about their wonderful leader, the lion. Of course that made him quite happy.

"Tell us," said the hippopotamus, who had a sled tied to each big foot, "how did you ever come to think of such a marvelous idea?"

"Oh, it was really quite easy for me," said the lion.
"You see—." But then for some strange reason he
stopped. And to the surprise of everyone including himself,
he said, "No . . . it wasn't my idea at all. It was the work
of a little gray mouse and his friend the elephant. And
now, on behalf of the village and on behalf of myself, I
must go and thank them."

But when he went to look for them, they were
nowhere to be found. There were only giant footprints
in the sugar snow that led off into the jungle.

All in all, it was a most unusual day.